STEP INTO READING®

STEP 3

MARC BROWN

ARTHUR
AND THE
SCHOOL PET

A Sticker Book

Random House 🏠 New York

www.stepintoreading.com
Educators and librarians, for a variety of teaching tools, visit us at
www.randomhouse.com/teachers
Library of Congress Cataloging-in-Publication Data
Brown, Marc Tolon.
Arthur and the school pet / by Marc Brown. p.   cm. — (Step into reading. A step 3 sticker book)
SUMMARY: D.W. volunteers to take care of the class gerbil during Christmas vacation and finds that he is difficult to keep track of.
ISBN 0-375-81001-3 (trade) — ISBN 0-375-91001-8 (lib. bdg.)
[1. Gerbils—Fiction. 2. Pets—Fiction. 3. Christmas—Fiction. 4. Vacations—Fiction.] I. Title.
II. Series: Step into reading sticker books. Step 3. PZ7.B81618 Aih 2003b [E]—dc21 2002015426
Printed in the United States of America 19 18 17 16 15 14 13
STEP INTO READING, RANDOM HOUSE, and the Random House colophon are registered trademarks of Random House, Inc. ARTHUR is a registered trademark of Marc Brown.

It was D.W.'s last day of school before Christmas vacation. "Who will take our gerbil home for the holidays?" Ms. Morgan asked.

"Not us!" said Tommy
and Timmy Tibble.
"Our grandmother said,
'Never again.'"
"I'll take him," said D.W.

"Great," said Ms. Morgan,
"but remember, Speedy is speedy."
"Oh, I'll be very careful," said D.W.

Arthur helped D.W.

carry Speedy home in his cage.

"He's cute," said Arthur.

"He's smart, too," said D.W.

"I'm going to teach him tricks."

"He's not a dog," said Arthur.

"You can't teach gerbils tricks."

D.W. kept Speedy in her room.
"You can't play with him, Arthur,"
she said. "He might get away."

But she played with him.

She tried to teach him

to stand on one paw.

"Be a ballerina," she told him,

"and I'll give you this cheese."

But Speedy just wanted

to eat the cheese.

On Christmas Eve,

D.W. put Speedy's cage

under the tree.

"Santa will bring a present

for Speedy, too," she said.

After D.W. went to bed,

Arthur put a piece of cheese

in Speedy's cage.

"Just in case Santa forgets,"

he said to himself.

The next morning, D.W. ran
to see what Santa had left her.
But the first thing she saw
was Speedy's cage.
It was empty!
"HELP!" she screamed.
"Speedy is gone!"

Everyone came running.

They looked under the sofa

and behind the presents

and all around the living room.

D.W. cried harder and harder.

Then Arthur looked up at the tree.

"Look!" shouted Arthur.

"Speedy's on top of the tree!"

He was eating a piece of cheese

and standing on one paw.

"Does he think he's a ballerina?"

laughed Arthur.

"Yes, Smarty-Pants," said D.W.

"I taught him that trick."

Somehow Speedy got out
of his cage three more times.
Once they found him
under the cake box.
He was eating carrot cake.

Once they found him
sleeping in D.W.'s dollhouse.

And once they found him
in Arthur's snow boot.

"I am so glad that school
starts tomorrow," said Mom.
"I need a vacation
from that gerbil."
"I want Speedy
to look very nice
when he goes back to school,"
said D.W.

"So I'm going to give him
a bubble bath."
When D.W. said "bath,"
Speedy took off
like lightning!

D.W. and Mom looked everywhere.

So did Arthur and Dad.

They looked upstairs.

They looked downstairs.

They looked in boxes

and drawers and closets.

But no one could find Speedy.

"I can never go to school again!"

cried D.W.

"Don't worry," said Arthur.

"He'll turn up."

But Arthur looked worried.

D.W. got ready for bed.

"Everyone is going to hate me
for losing Speedy," she said.

Then she crawled under the covers.

She felt something warm and furry.

"Speedy!" she whispered.
And there he was—
hiding in her bed!

D.W. arrived at school
with Speedy in his cage.
"Was he much trouble?"
asked Ms. Morgan.
"No problem," said D.W.